To

This book belongs to:

_____

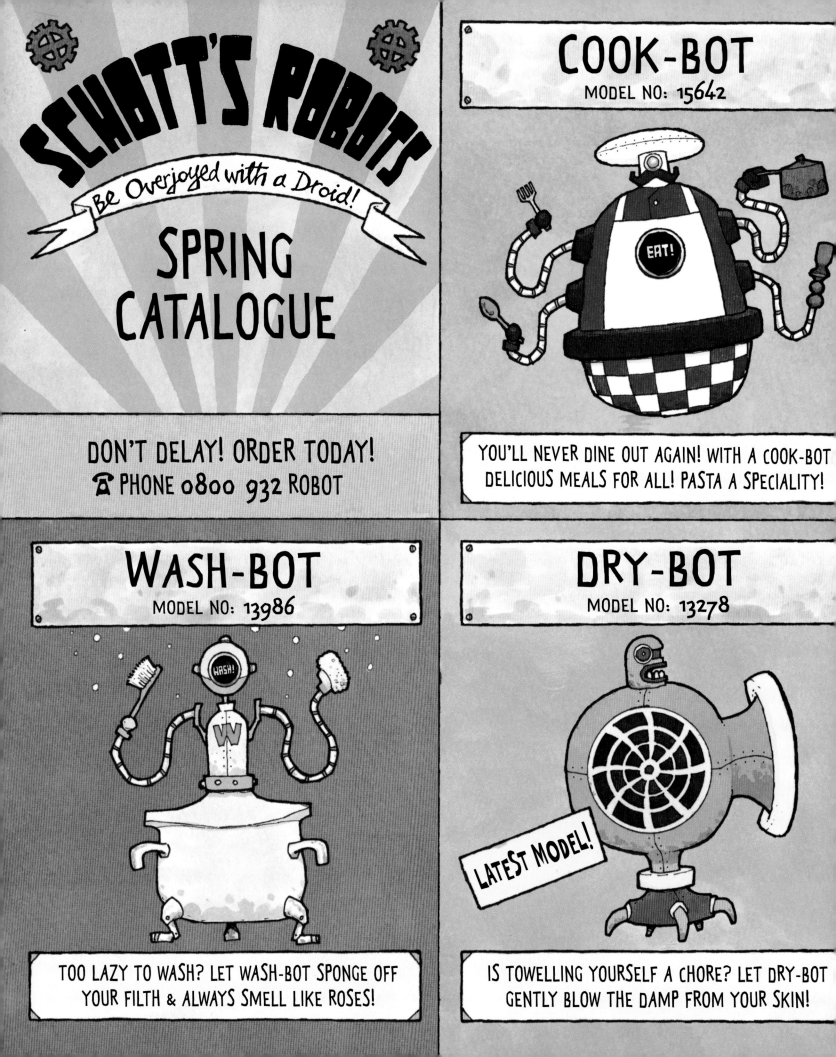

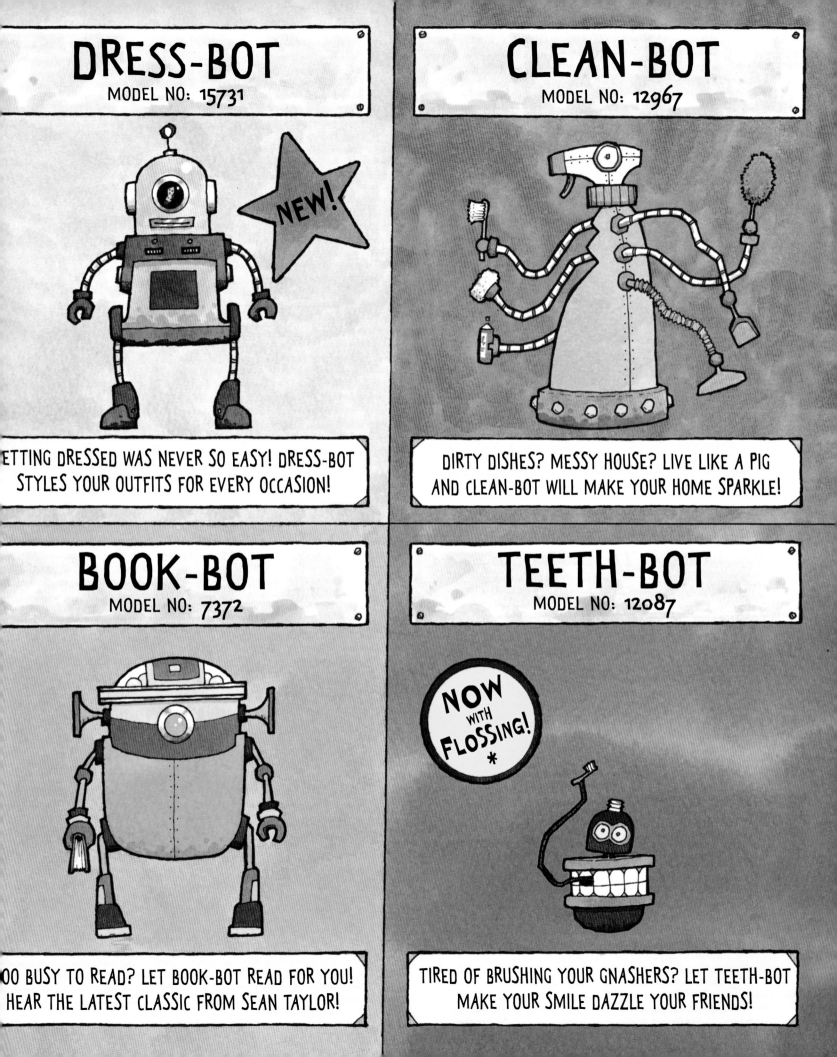

DRESS-BOT
MODEL NO: 15731

NEW!

ETTING DRESSED WAS NEVER SO EASY! DRESS-BOT STYLES YOUR OUTFITS FOR EVERY OCCASION!

CLEAN-BOT
MODEL NO: 12967

DIRTY DISHES? MESSY HOUSE? LIVE LIKE A PIG AND CLEAN-BOT WILL MAKE YOUR HOME SPARKLE!

BOOK-BOT
MODEL NO: 7372

OO BUSY TO READ? LET BOOK-BOT READ FOR YOU! HEAR THE LATEST CLASSIC FROM SEAN TAYLOR!

TEETH-BOT
MODEL NO: 12087

NOW WITH FLOSSING! *

TIRED OF BRUSHING YOUR GNASHERS? LET TEETH-BOT MAKE YOUR SMILE DAZZLE YOUR FRIENDS!

For Fidelma and Tony – S.T.

For Hal & Ida – R.C.

This paperback first published in 2014 by Andersen Press Ltd.
First published in Great Britain in 2013 by Andersen Press Ltd.,
20 Vauxhall Bridge Road, London SW1V 2SA.
Published in Australia by Random House Australia Pty.,
Level 3, 100 Pacific Highway, North Sydney, NSW 2060.
Text copyright © Sean Taylor, 2013.
Illustration copyright © Ross Collins, 2013.
The rights of Sean Taylor and Ross Collins to be identified as the
author and illustrator of this work have been asserted by them
in accordance with the Copyright, Designs and Patents Act, 1988.
All rights reserved.
Colour separated in Switzerland by Photolitho AG, Zürich.
Printed and bound in Malaysia by Tien Wah Press.

10   9   8   7   6   5   4   3   2   1

British Library Cataloguing in Publication Data available.

ISBN 978 1 84939 660 8

MIX
Paper from
responsible sources
FSC
www.fsc.org   FSC® C012700

My mum and dad are busy.
So just last night they said,
"We decided to buy these fantastic robots
to get you into bed."

I thought they must be joking.
But Dad switched the robots on.
Mum said, "They're the latest models.
What could *possibly* go wrong?"

Then Cook-bot made spaghetti.
I ate the lot off my plate.

Clean-bot did the washing-up.
Everything seemed just great.

Wash-bot ran a bath.
It said, "YOU WILL BE SPICK AND SPAN."
I got my bath toys down off the shelf.
But that's when the rumpus began.

Crocodile is my favourite toy.
His teeth can really snap.
But soon as Wash-bot spotted him,
it got in a bit of a flap.

It said, "DANGEROUS ANIMAL IN THE WATER!"

Three warning-lights flashed red.

Then it went and slipped into Dress-bot,

who sat down on Teeth-bot's head.

Dress-bot turned round and round
like it didn't know what to do.

And Teeth-bot started brushing its head
and squirting toothpaste down the loo.

Clean-bot was whizzing about.
It was trying to keep things tidy.

But Dress-bot started putting pyjamas on the robot that had to dry me.

Cook-bot came in and stared.
And its warning-lights flashed too.
Then it nodded and zoomed away
like it knew just what to do.

I hoped it could sort out the mess.
This was getting beyond a laugh.
But all it did was cook more spaghetti
and tip it into the bath.

I know that robots can't cry,
But Clean-bot looked close to tears.

Book-bot sat with a book on the bed,
and smoke coming out its ears.

And Dry-bot couldn't manage to get my pyjamas off its head.

So, in the end, I left them
and got **myself** into bed.

I think the robots were exhausted.
They crashed around some more.
Then everything went quiet until . . .

The place was a bit of a mess.
It hadn't worked quite like they'd said.
And I don't think they got a good night's sleep . . .

AAAAARGH!!!!

With SEVEN ROBOTS IN THEIR BED!

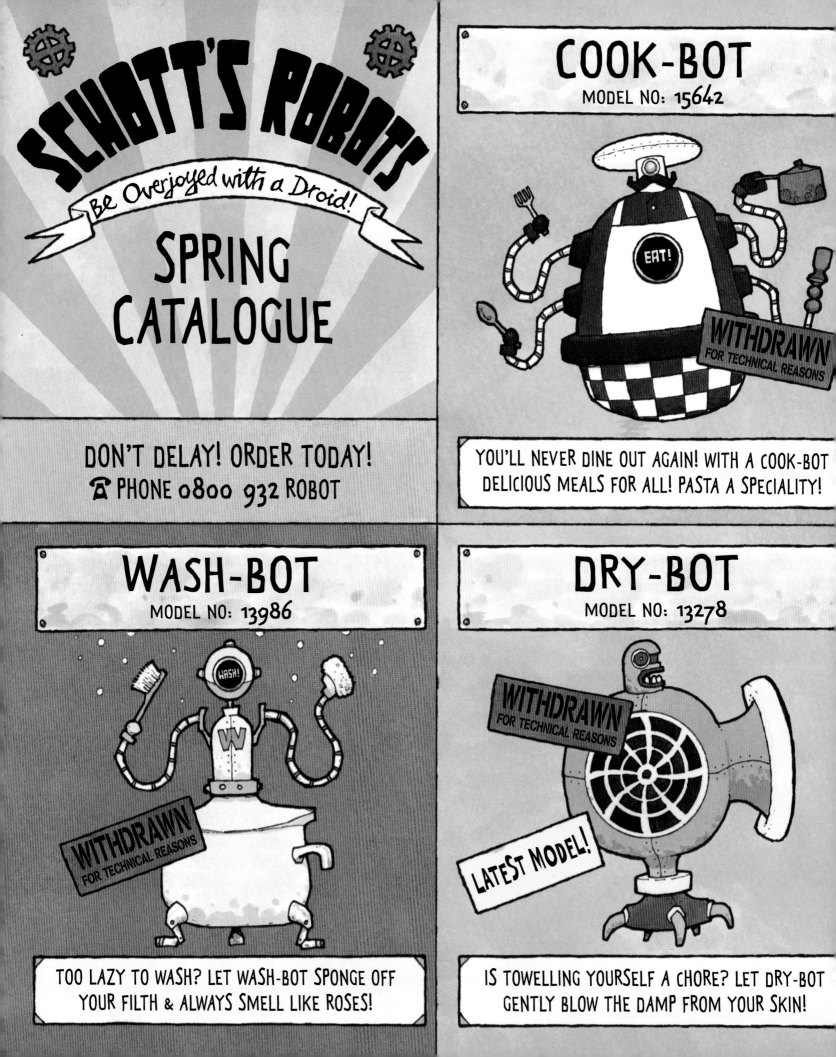

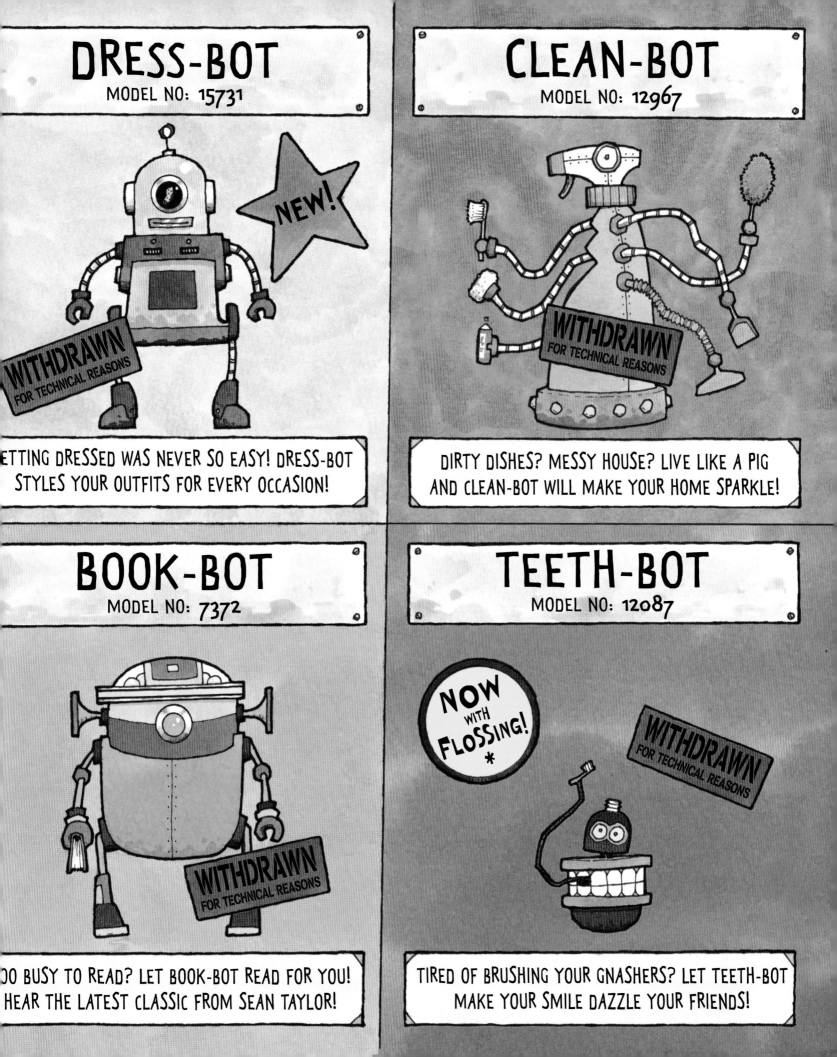

DRESS-BOT
MODEL NO: 15731

NEW!

WITHDRAWN
FOR TECHNICAL REASONS

ETTING DRESSED WAS NEVER SO EASY! DRESS-BOT
STYLES YOUR OUTFITS FOR EVERY OCCASION!

CLEAN-BOT
MODEL NO: 12967

WITHDRAWN
FOR TECHNICAL REASONS

DIRTY DISHES? MESSY HOUSE? LIVE LIKE A PIG
AND CLEAN-BOT WILL MAKE YOUR HOME SPARKLE!

BOOK-BOT
MODEL NO: 7372

WITHDRAWN
FOR TECHNICAL REASONS

OO BUSY TO READ? LET BOOK-BOT READ FOR YOU!
HEAR THE LATEST CLASSIC FROM SEAN TAYLOR!

TEETH-BOT
MODEL NO: 12087

NOW
WITH
FLOSSING!
*

WITHDRAWN
FOR TECHNICAL REASONS

TIRED OF BRUSHING YOUR GNASHERS? LET TEETH-BOT
MAKE YOUR SMILE DAZZLE YOUR FRIENDS!

Also illustrated by Ross Collins:

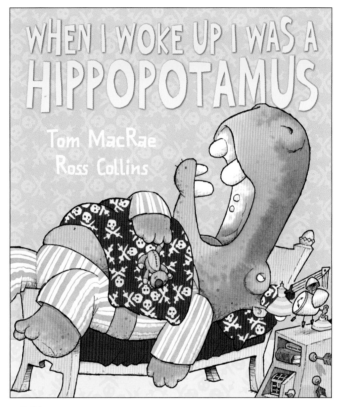

9781849393591